uniquely

WRITTEN BY JOYCE MEYER

ILLUSTRATED BY Marcin Piwowarski

WORTHY
kids™

ISBN: 978-1-5460-1248-1

WorthyKids
Hachette Book Group
1290 Avenue of the Americas
New York, NY 10104

Library of Congress Cataloging-in-Publication Data
Names: Meyer, Joyce. | Piwowarski, Marcin, illustrator.
Title: Uniquely you / by Joyce Meyer ; art by Marcin Piwowarski.
Description: New York, NY : WorthyKids, [2022] | Audience: Ages 4-7. |
   Summary: Encourages children to embrace and celebrate their wonderfully
   unique God-given identities.
Identifiers: LCCN 2021046235 | ISBN 9781546012481 (hardback)
Subjects: CYAC: Individuality—Fiction. | Christian life—Fiction. | LCGFT:
   Picture books.
Classification: LCC PZ7.M57171 Un 2022 | DDC [E]—dc23
LC record available at https://lccn.loc.gov/2021046235

Designed by Melissa Reagan

Printed and bound in U.S.A.
PHX
10 9 8 7 6 5 4 3 2 1

I praise you because I am
fearfully and wonderfully made;
your works are wonderful,
I know that full well.

—Psalm 139:14 NIV

Did you know? Have you heard?
GOD made YOU.
And there is no one else in this GREAT BIG
WORLD who is exactly like you.

You're one of a kind,
an original, UNIQUE!
You are a MASTERPIECE made by
the One who scattered the stars
and hung the moon.

From your wiggly toes

to the tip of your nose,

GOD made you who

He wanted you to be.

And you make Him so HAPPY
that He just has to sing!

GOD loves you with a love that
ZOOMS past forever—
and NEVER, EVER ENDS.

And He wants you to love yourself too.
Not in a way that's selfish or unkind.
But with a love that says,
"I'm AWESOME and AMAZING,
because that's the way
GOD MADE ME!"

You may not be perfect,

but God doesn't expect you to be.
You'll MESS UP and MAKE MISTAKES.

And sometimes you'll choose to do wrong.

God doesn't stop loving you. No, not even then.

Instead, He'll use **HIS WORD** to show you

how to make things right again—

because **GOD'S GOT PLANS FOR YOU!**

God created you for a reason.
He's filled your heart
with **HOPES** and **DREAMS**
and all kinds of important things
He wants you to do.

And He's given you gifts—
every **TALENT** and **ABILITY**
you need—to get those things done.

If you're wondering what your GIFTS might be,
think about the things you love to do—
the things no one else can do quite like you.

Are you a whiz with NUMBERS
and MATH?

Are you a wonder with WORDS?

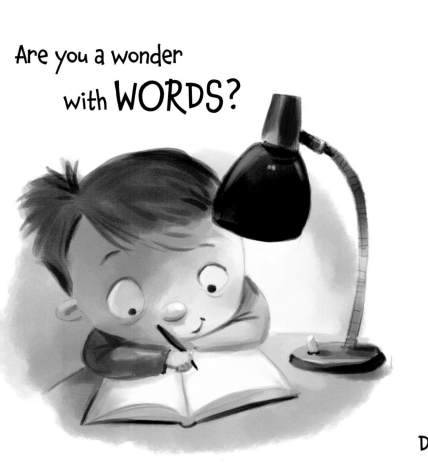

Do you PAINT the clouds?

Or shine like a star on the SOCCER FIELD or the STAGE?

Are you extra good at helping, sharing, or CHEERING others on?

Or maybe you're marvelous
at MAKING FRIENDS
and welcoming others in.

We each have a GIFT from God,
and each gift is WONDERFUL in its own way.

But our gifts are DIFFERENT.

They aren't quite the same.

They're as UNIQUE as
YOU and ME.

That's because **GOD LOVES VARIETY**—
infinite and endless!

Just look at the FLOWERS.
Look at the TREES.

Look at the oceans filled with DOLPHINS and STARFISH and ANEMONES.

You might wish you had SOMEONE ELSE'S GIFT.

You might dream about doing the things they can do.

And you might even PRETEND that you can.

But remember, God didn't create others to be like you, and He didn't create you to be like them.

Use the gifts GOD has given YOU—and let Him AMAZE THE WORLD through you.

It won't always be easy.
Sometimes it will be **TOUGH**.
It takes **COURAGE** to be yourself.

Some people might think you're silly.
Others might whisper that you're weird.
And there might be people who decide
they don't want to be your friend.
If that happens, SMILE and be KIND.

Then be on the lookout for TRUE FRIENDS.
Here's a hint: they'll be the ones who cheer
when you're being the most UNIQUELY YOU.

GOD wants you
to SPARKLE,

and He wants you
to SHINE.

He wants you to be happy
BEING YOU—

and to **HELP OTHERS** learn to love Him
and love themselves too.

So be BOLD and be BRAVE—
and dare to be WONDERFULLY,
MARVELOUSLY,
UNIQUELY